Katie in London

James Mayhew

For Max
~ a story about your Mum ~

ORCHARD BOOKS
338 Euston Road, London, NW1 3BH
Orchard Books Australia
Level 17/207 Kent Street, Sydney, NSW 2000

First published in 2003 by Orchard Books
First published in paperback in 2004

This edition published in 2012

ISBN 978 1 40832 385 4

Text and illustrations © James Mayhew 2003

The right of James Mayhew to be identified as the author and illustrator
of this book has been asserted by him in accordance with the
Copyright, Designs and Patents Act, 1988.

A CIP catalogue record for this book is available from the British Library.

2 4 6 8 10 9 7 5 3 1

Printed in China

Orchard Books is a division of Hachette Children's Books,
an Hachette UK company.
www.hachette.co.uk

London seemed very big to Katie. Big trains, big buildings and big crowds. She held on to Grandma with one hand and her little brother, Jack, with the other. They all got on to a big red bus and set off to see the sights.

But when they got off at Trafalgar Square, Grandma was tired.
"I'll just have a little rest," she yawned. "You two stay by that lion,
then I'll know where you are."

Katie climbed on to the big bronze lion and pulled Jack up after her.

As the sun came out, the lion seemed to turn from grey to gold.

"Do you mind?" said a very deep voice. It was the lion! "Who said you could clamber all over me?" he asked.

"We're very sorry," said Katie. "Grandma said to stay with you."

"Then I suppose you must," sighed the lion. "Now, what shall we do?"

"We wanted to see the sights, but Grandma fell asleep," said Katie. "Can you take us?"

"Oh yes, please do!" said Jack.

The lion shook his mane.
"Hold on tight!" he roared,
bounding out of Trafalgar Square.

My goodness, how people stared! But the lion didn't mind. "This is much better than lying on that stone all day," he said. "You have no idea how cold my tummy gets. Now, where shall we go?"

"You choose!" yelled Katie and Jack.

The lion took them to St Paul's Cathedral first.
They gazed up at the enormous dome.

"It makes me feel very small," said Jack.

"It makes me feel very dizzy," laughed
the lion, "but off we must go as
there's still so much to see!"

Next, the lion took Katie and Jack to an old castle.

"The Tower of London," said the lion. "Ghosts of kings and queens haunt the towers!"

Katie shivered and held Jack's hand.

"Don't worry, they only come out after midnight," said the lion. "But you can see their jewels and crowns."

The Crown Jewels were in a small, special room. It was quite a tight squeeze for the lion. The jewels sparkled like stars in a night sky, but in all sorts of colours – green emeralds, red rubies and blue sapphires.

Afterwards, the lion pretended he was a ghost and chased Katie and Jack.

"Excuse me," called a man in an old-fashioned costume, "but you're scaring my ravens!"

"Who's he?" whispered Katie.

"He's a Yeoman Warder," said the lion. "He thinks that the towers will fall down if the ravens leave. I think it's time to go!"

The lion decided to carry
them across the River Thames.
They trotted on to Tower Bridge.
Suddenly an alarm sounded
and lights flashed.

A boat was coming and the bridge was opening to let it through. **"STOP!"** yelled Katie. But the lion didn't stop – he jumped!

But instead of landing on the other side, they landed on the boat. They chugged along the river, passing great ships and going under dark bridges.

"Look! That's the Globe Theatre," said the lion. "Shakespeare wrote some fine plays that are performed there, although very few of them have lions in them."

"What's that big wheel over there?" asked Jack.

"It must be the London Eye," said Katie. "Why don't we go on it?"

"You don't expect me to go on that thing do you?" said the lion, as they all jumped off the boat.

Before the lion could say another word, Katie bustled him on board the London Eye.

Slowly the wheel turned and they rose high above London. The poor lion turned rather pale and began to shake, but soon even he couldn't help enjoying the view. He pointed to Big Ben. "Goodness, it's nearly eleven o'clock. We must hurry!"

As they came down, Big Ben chimed eleven times. Katie and Jack jumped on to the lion and they raced across a bridge, past the huge clock and the Houses of Parliament.

They hopped in and out of queues of traffic, past taxis and red double-decker buses, past parks and grand buildings. They could hear music and drums.

"It's the Changing of the Guard!" said the lion. "Follow me – left, right, left, right…"

The lion marched off behind the guardsmen, in time to the music. Katie and Jack followed, all the way to the gates of Buckingham Palace.

"Sorry," said a policeman, "only Royal
Guards are allowed through here."
So Katie and Jack jumped upon the
lion and he walked on, past the palace.

They hoped to see a real prince or princess. Instead, they noticed a lot of flags and crests with lions on them. The lion smiled. "I'm very well-known by the Royal Family."

"Why is that?" asked Katie.

"Because the lion is called the King of the Beasts!" said the lion proudly.

And as they galloped away, perhaps they did catch a glimpse of someone waving from a palace window?

By now the lion's paws were beginning to ache, so they all went to sit in a leafy park. The lion dangled his paws in a cool lake. Jack bought ice creams with his pocket money.

"Delicious!" said the lion. "I love tutti-frutti!"

"How are your paws?" asked Katie.

"Rather sore," admitted the lion. "I'm not used to all this walking. Perhaps we can catch a bus back to Trafalgar Square?"

A policeman told them to catch a number nine bus from Harrods, the big department store.

"I wish I didn't have to go back," said the lion, sadly.

"Don't you like Trafalgar Square?" asked Katie.

"Of course," said the lion, "but I do get such a very cold tummy lying on the stone all the time."

Jack whispered in Katie's ear and they both smiled. They went inside Harrods, and came out a few minutes later with a small parcel.

Then they jumped on to the bus and travelled back to Trafalgar Square.

"This is for you," said Jack, handing the parcel from Harrods to the lion. "We bought it with the last of our pocket money." The lion unwrapped it and laughed. "It's a woolly blanket!"

"It's to keep your tummy warm," said Katie.
"How kind you are," sighed the lion.
"Thanks for showing us London," said Jack.
"Next time I'll show you even more!" said the lion.

Then Katie saw Grandma was waking up.
The lion hopped on to his stone and kept
very still. And, as the sun went in, he
turned from gold to grey.

"Hello, you two," said Grandma.
"Shall we go off to see the sights now?"

"Oh!" said Katie. "I'm much too tired."

"I need a rest!" said Jack.
And they both flopped down on
a bench and fell asleep.

More fun facts about some of the sights on Katie and Jack's tour!

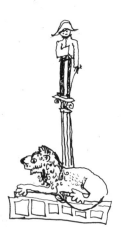

Trafalgar Square and Nelson's Column

Nelson's Column stands in the centre of Trafalgar Square, with four proud, bronze lions sitting at its base. The lions were designed by Sir Edwin Landseer, and have guarded Nelson since 1867. Don't forget to visit the National Gallery on the north side of Trafalgar Square.

London Eye

This enormous Ferris wheel was built to celebrate the Millennium, but still stands alongside the Thames and has proved to be one of London's most popular attractions. Its capsules are able to carry up to 15,000 visitors a day, on a 30 minute ride called a 'flight'. On a clear day you can see up to 25 miles in every direction – sometimes you can even see Windsor Castle.

Tower of London and Tower Bridge

The Tower has served many purposes in its long history – a royal residence, a prison, a zoo, a mint, and a safe place to store the Crown Jewels. Join a tour by one of the Yeoman Warders, or Beefeaters, and learn all about the Tower's history – good and bad! Tower Bridge has stood next to the Tower of London since 1894. If you are lucky, you may see the bridge open to let a boat pass up the River Thames!

Buckingham Palace and the Changing of the Guards

Buckingham Palace is the official London residence of Her Majesty The Queen. The Changing of the Guard is a spectacular ceremony which takes place inside the palace gates at 11.30am, daily in summer and alternate days for the rest of the year. Arrive early to make sure you get the best view, and see the soldiers march past in their traditional full regimental uniform.